THE COWBOY'S BRIDE
COURAGE COUNTY BRIDES

MIA BRODY

This is a work of fiction. Names, characters, places, and incidents either are the product of the author's imagination or are used fictitiously. Any resemblance to actual persons, living or dead, events, or locales is entirely coincidental.

Copyright © 2022 by Mia Brody

All rights reserved. No part of this book may be reproduced or used in any manner without written permission of the author except for the use of quotations in a book review.

1
RANGER

Grieving isn't a spectator event. At least, it's not for me. The last of the funeral guests haven't even left yet and I'm already wheeling myself back to my office. Work is my sanctuary, and I desperately need the respite it offers me today.

People think that running a ranch is all about cowboys doing manual labor. Wrangling bulls and shit. They don't realize that a ranch is a business. It's as much strategy and planning as having the physical strength to repair a fence. Any idiot can do that.

In my office, I spot the envelope with the familiar messy scrawl on it. Grandpa didn't have good motor control in the final years of his life, but he was still cognitively here and present with us.

Through failed crops, economic recessions, and even the loss of his own son, the man never gave up. He kept this ranch going and now, it's my turn to keep the Scott family legacy alive.

I blink away the tears as I trace my fingertips along his script. I don't have to pull out the letter to know what it says.

Grandpa was a diehard romantic. A man who believed in forever and soulmates. Now he's making marriage a condition for inheriting the family ranch. If my seven brothers and I want to keep this place in our name, we have no choice but to accept our coming nuptials.

There's a knock on the door and when I call out, Ethan and Logan enter the room. Like all of my siblings, these two are my foster brothers. I didn't care much for them at first. But they've had my back more times than I can count.

"You ducked out on us," Logan announces as he takes a seat across from me. He sets his muddy boots on my desk.

I gesture to the spreadsheet open on my computer screen as if I were busy working. Even cowboys have to do paperwork. At least, you have to if you hope to keep the place operating lawfully. "Had some figures to look at."

Ethan says nothing as he takes the seat beside Logan. He's never been particularly chatty but after finding out his wife was cheating on him in front of the whole town, he's gotten even quieter. Sometimes, it's downright unnerving.

"Did you need something?" I prompt when neither of them say anything. Ethan's silence I'm used to, but Logan is usually talkative no matter what.

Logan clears his throat. "We're not going to have to leave now, are we?"

It's a question only a foster kid would ask, and my heart breaks for the second time since Grandpa passed away. My brothers and I have seen enough cruelty and pain to last a lifetime. We all came to the Scott ranch at different times, but a brotherhood has formed over the years. The eight of us mind as well be blood at this point.

"The ranch is legally ours as long as we fulfill the terms of the will," I reassure him.

Ethan narrows his gaze. Trust him to pick up on my careful wording. None of my brothers know about the upcoming marriages yet. The will won't officially be read until two days from now. But Grandpa and I were close. Maybe that's why he left me a letter and not the others. "What do you mean the terms of the will?"

I work to keep my voice even and unaffected. I've already had three days to process this news and even then, it still tastes sour. "In order to inherit, each of the Scott siblings must marry. Grandpa has signed us up for a mail order bride matchmaking service."

"You're shitting me," Ethan says, rage coloring his tone.

"All you have to do is finish filling out a profile and select a compatible match." I've done the research and the company that Grandpa selected is highly reputable. He even gave them the deposits already. Hell, he did everything but handpick the women for us.

"Wait a second, I get that he wants us to find our *soulmates*." Logan emphasizes the word with obvious disgust. "But what if we sacrificed a few of us? We draw straws and those guys have to get married while the rest of us are free."

I chuckle at his suggestion of sacrificing a few of us. Trust Love 'Em and Leave 'Em Logan to look at marriage that way. "I've already talked to the lawyer. There will be no exceptions and no loopholes. Anyone who doesn't marry doesn't get their share.

Their portion of the land will be sold to the highest bidder at auction."

Ethan lets out a blue streak under his breath. We all know that keeping the ranch whole is the only way to ensure it survives. It was a sneaky move that gives my grandfather the last word.

Logan blows out a breath. "Dammit, the Scott brothers are about to get hitched."

I reach for the good bourbon I keep in the bottom drawer and pour the three of us a generous amount. "Here's to the end of the bachelorhood."

A WEEK LATER, I ROLL INTO THE BEDROOM I'VE prepared for my soon-to-be bride. Just the thought makes me uneasy. How desperate is this woman that she'd marry a man sight unseen?

As soon as the will was read, everything was already set-in motion. The only thing I had to do was sign on the dotted line, agreeing to the contract marriage. I received a brief profile to review but no picture. The same as my future wife.

With my good hand, I run my fingertips across my face. The muscle spasms have been worse than usual thanks to the stress of my upcoming wedding. I already know I look like I'm scowling.

I haven't talked to the heavens since I was a kid in high school who spent just about every day bullied because he looked different. But today, I can't help turning my face toward the ceiling. "Would you send me someone plain?"

If I'm being honest, I want more than a roommate or a companion. I want a real marriage, a wife that will build a future with me.

Experience has taught me that beautiful women don't look twice at men like me. But maybe if she were plain, she wouldn't be turned off by my appearance and obvious disability. Maybe she'd be willing to give me a chance.

"I want a real wife. Kids too if you'll give 'em to me," I admit. I've accepted that I'm alone. But so many nights, I finish my work for the ranch, drive home, and wish that there were lights on. A happy wife and playful children waiting to greet me. Maybe this is my chance to finally have that.

Tia

"Just look for the man with the dogwood bouquet," I repeat to myself as I follow the other passengers off the plane. It was my first plane ride and if I have anything to say about it, my final one too. I don't ever want to encounter turbulence like that again.

Agreeing to become a mail-order bride isn't something I thought I'd do. The matchmaking company was reliable, and all of my costs were paid by the groom. Now all I have to do is show up and hope he doesn't reject me.

I don't know what I'll do if that happens, and bile threatens to climb my throat. I ran away from home three nights ago on the eve of my eighteenth birthday. It was either that or become the sixth wife of Prophet. Prophet who's already married my older two sisters. One of them disappeared and the other is a shell of her former self.

It was Sarah, a local librarian, who sheltered me and helped me get out. When I found the matchmaking service, she encouraged me to try it. Her husband promised that men on the outside are different. They don't believe in punishing their wives and terrorizing their children.

I had to lie on the forms when I sent them in. I said I was twenty-one. But still I've waited until I was eighteen. At least then the marriage will be legal, and it'll be harder for my father to drag me back to "the community".

It's a funny word to describe a little strip of land in the mountains of Georgia where we all live in houses that look just alike. We dress alike and go to the same tiny church where Prophet shares the latest revelation he's been gifted with.

Please don't let my father come for me. I take a deep breath and remind myself that my future husband doesn't want to be greeted by a panicked wife. I have to make this marriage work, and that means pasting a happy smile on my face.

Scanning the Asheville airport terminal, I feel the familiar overwhelm crash into me. When you've spent your life hidden away in the community, the world outside of it feels big and scary. I don't think I've ever seen this many people and they're all bumping into me and carrying on their way.

For a moment, I'm convinced I made a terrible mistake. I want to go home. I want to be where everything is familiar. Then I remind myself of the way my sister looks now. Pale, gaunt, covered in bruises. *I won't let that be me.*

I tried to get her to come with me, but she wouldn't. I had to leave on my own and now it's time to figure out how to do this, how to become part of the outside world.

Shoulders squared, I tell myself to take this one moment at a time as I look around, searching for a man with a bouquet. There's one guy but he's holding white roses as a woman in an Army uniform throws herself into his arms.

Will it be like that after we've been married for a while? Will I get someone who likes to bring me flowers and wants me to throw myself into his arms?

Then I spot him, and it feels like time stands still. There's a man sitting in a motorized wheelchair with a bouquet of dogwood blooms in his hand. Something deep in my gut tells me this is him, my future husband.

The dating profile never mentioned a wheelchair. It seems a strange detail to leave out about the man.

He lifts his face as if sensing my gaze and his scowl has me taking a half-step back. He looks angry and I've spent my life around angry men. Men who would punish a woman or child for the slightest sin. *Please don't be the angry type.*

I study his features. His dark hair and nearly black gaze have me thinking of a raven. I can't help the shiver that runs down my spine as soon as I make the connection. Before she left, Mom always said that ravens are an ill omen, a warning of loss to come.

He smiles at me. At least, I think he tries to. It softens his features a little, but it doesn't ease the churning in my stomach.

I approach him cautiously, prepared to bolt. Sarah told me I could call her anytime. She even gave me a smartphone. It's the first electronic device I've had in my whole life. *If this turns into a bad situation, you can always call her.*

"Are you Ranger? I'm Re—Tia," I quickly correct myself. It's going to take time to learn to introduce myself as Tia. I left Rebecca, my birth name, behind. It felt too close to my past and I wanted a fresh start. The name Tia means happiness and joy. I figure I could use both of those things in my life now.

"These are for you," he shoves the flowers at me. "We need to get on the road if we're going to beat the snowstorm. Do you have bags with you?"

I hold up my black duffel bag. Running away from home in the middle of the night means I don't have much. If it hadn't been for Sarah, I wouldn't have anything at all. "Just this."

We stand there staring awkwardly at each other for a moment and I don't know what to do. Am I supposed to hug him or something?

He grunts. "Follow me then."

Without another word, he pushes a button on his chair and starts down the terminal without waiting. Disappointment lances through me at the cold reception as I think about the soldier and the way her man greeted her so warmly. *I'm marrying a man who doesn't like me.*

2
RANGER

Another unanswered prayer. This woman isn't plain. She's damn beautiful with long, dark hair the flows halfway down her back and mossy green eyes that are filled with disappointment. There's no mistaking it. This will be a marriage in name only.

"Did you say there would be a snowstorm?" She asks when I'm in the driver's seat of my truck. Wheelchair accessible trucks aren't cheap, but nothing beats the feeling of freedom that comes with being able to drive myself around town.

I risk a glance at her as I start the ignition. There's something about her. She seems skittish. Maybe it has to do with the fact that we're strangers who are getting married. If I knew how, I'd try to comfort her. But I've never really spent much time around women, unless you count Mrs. Scott. "If we stay on time, we won't get caught in it."

"I don't like storms," she murmurs, turning her face to stare out the passenger window. She wraps her arms around herself, looking tiny and defenseless in the cab of my big truck. It only reminds me of how young she is. The profile I received says she's twenty-one, but she looks even younger than that. Still, the matchmaking agency assured us that every potential bride is of legal age.

I reach for something to ask her as I merge with the traffic onto the interstate. But as much as I try to recall her profile, I'm drawing a blank. What does a man say to his future wife?

After forty minutes of silence, she shifts in her seat. The simple motion draws my attention to her shapely legs that are tucked under a white skirt with pink flowers on it. I hate that I notice the fact or even care about it.

"We're going to the courthouse first, right?"

I should probably offer to stop for lunch first since it's a long drive to Courage County. But if she's half as nervous about this upcoming marriage as I am, there's no way she's in the mood to eat. "That's the plan."

"Good," she visibly sags with relief. "I'd rather get

it over with."

Yeah, there's no happy wife and playful children in my future. At least, she's making this obvious early on. Now I can't help but wonder if she's not looking for a real marriage, why she's here.

Tia

"A WEDDING CAN BE A HAPPY THING," I TRY TO convince myself as I look in the mirror of the courthouse bathroom. With shaking hands, I reach for a tube of pink lipstick. I've never owned makeup until a few months ago. Sarah has slowly introduced it to me, teaching me how to wear it.

Even then, I could only wear it when no one would see. So, I'd put it on during the days when I was allowed to leave the community to go to the local library. I was supposed to be reading the children religious tracts that Prophet wrote. But I'd spend the afternoons reading them fairytales instead.

Please don't be like Prophet. I silently beg Ranger as I take one last look at myself in the mirror. I just want a sweet marriage to a good man. Someone who can love me and that I love in return.

Ranger would barely talk to me in the car. I'm not sure if he doesn't like me or I make him uncomfortable. It could be both.

When I've stalled for as long as I possibly can, I square my shoulders and leave the bathroom. My heart is pounding a million miles a minute and my palms are clammy.

Marriage isn't a good thing for a woman where I come from. It's something that means being controlled and manipulated.

I want my marriage to be like Sarah's. Her husband worships the ground she walks on. His every thought is focused on how to make her feel loved and secure. It's obvious with one look at the man that he adores his wife.

Maybe Ranger will be that kind of husband once he gets to know me. The thought eases my nerves and makes me feel slightly better. It's possible we'll just have a rough beginning, right?

Ranger is waiting outside the courtroom, glancing between his watch and the glass doors that showcase the rapidly darkening sky. "Are you ready?"

I manage a nod and wait for him to say something else. When he doesn't, I try for a compliment. "You look…nice." I started to say handsome, the way Sarah always calls her husband that. But the word seems a bit much when we don't know each other.

Before he can say anything, the court doors are swinging open and a little old lady is welcoming us inside. Her eyes are sparkling and there's kindness in her blue gaze. She pats her white perm. "Are y'all ready to get married?"

Ranger audibly gulps at the same time I give her a smile that feels more like a grimace.

She leads us into the court room, and I expect to see a judge sitting there. Instead, the woman offers me a hearty handshake. "Hello, Tia, I'm Judge Helen. We're glad to have you joining the Courage County family."

This sweet little old lady who looks like she's about one second away from knitting me a sweater and baking a batch of cookies is the one in charge.

The idea of a woman in leadership is so strange to me. Back in the community, I was taught that women can't be leaders because we were deceived by the snake. That means a woman's judgement can never be trusted.

"Are y'all going for the traditional vows?" She

addresses the question to Ranger as two more court employees enter the room to be our witnesses.

"Yes, ma'am," he says in a quiet tone.

She asks us to join hands, but I feel weird towering over Ranger who's in his motorized wheelchair. So I pause to grab a chair with a blue cushion, dragging it over. I sit across from him, my knees pressed closely together.

He takes my hand then, his fingers rough against my soft ones. He's used to working hard with his hands. Still his touch is gentle and warm. I search his face, hoping to see those same qualities reflected on it. But I can't read his onyx gaze or figure out what he's thinking. Shouldn't we able to communicate with a look? Isn't that something married people can do?

Judge Helen launches into the vows. She's using traditional vows I've heard all my life. Except there's no promise to obey Ranger in them or mention of how he's the head of the household and I'll submit to him. It's foreign to me but I don't question it. I wanted a normal marriage. Maybe this is what it looks like on the outside.

When we're done, she says he can kiss the bride. Ranger leans forward and presses his lips to mine.

It's a quick peck that's over before it even began. Just like that, I get my first kiss. It might be the only kiss we ever share if the look on Ranger's face is anything to go by. He doesn't look like he enjoyed that at all.

We have to sign the marriage certificate after the ceremony. I grip the pen tightly as I sign my name and hope that no one notices the way my hand shakes. I've done it now. I've tied my life to a complete stranger's.

The drive to Ranger's ranch is a quiet one. I hope that he'll start talking and asking me questions, but he doesn't. Since I figure maybe he's the shy, quiet type, I decide to go first. "What size is the Scott Ranch?"

I remember from what I read that he's one of eight brothers. They all work together to keep the ranch running. Laney, the matchmaker who runs the agency that specializes in finding compatible matches for cowboys in rural locations, said the Scott Ranch is the second largest in the state. But to a girl who doesn't know anything about cowboys, that doesn't mean a whole lot.

"Big."

Ranger's short reply might be off-putting to some, but I'm willing to try again. "And you and your brothers run it together?"

"Yep."

So far, he hasn't told me anything I don't know. "Are you close to them?"

"Yep." A muscle in his jaw tics and his grip on the steering wheel tightens.

Finally, I accept that Ranger just isn't interested in talking to me. Maybe he'll be different when we're at his place. But I don't have high hopes. He hasn't had more than a sentence to say to me. He doesn't ask me questions about myself. He barely even kissed me.

He turns his truck down an unmarked dirt road that's blocked off with a gate. He quickly punches in a security code, but he has to do it twice, pausing to shake out his hand.

"Almost home," he mutters as the gate swings open. I'm not sure which of us he's talking to, so I don't respond.

He takes another winding dirt road and drives for several long minutes before pulling to a stop in front of a small, one-story home. The low-pitched roof with wide eaves and a chimney on the side looks like something out of a fairytale book I'd read the children. "You live here?"

"Yep."

If I'm going to stay here, I'll have to work on this man's vocabulary. I don't believe you should change the person you're with, but I'm pretty sure I can't endure a lifetime of one-word answers.

He leads me inside the house, stopping in the foyer. It's an open concept floorplan, so I can see the living room, kitchen, and dining room all at once. I survey the white walls that are decorated with large nature photographs.

Before I can ask about them, Ranger clears his throat. He points in each direction as he says, "Living room. Kitchen. Dining room. Dinner is in the fridge if you want to heat it up. I'm going to bed."

I blink. It's the most he's said to me since we've met.

He frowns down at his clenched fist before saying in a rush, "Your bedroom is down the hall. Second door on the left. The bathroom is beside it."

Then without another word or waiting for a response from me, Ranger pushes a button on his wheelchair and rolls down the hall and into a room. I listen as the door clicks shut.

"So this is married life," I whisper, wrapping my arms around myself. If I thought I was lonely on the plane or in the airport when I was surrounded by people, it's nothing compared to how forlorn I feel now.

3
TIA

I start by exploring the kitchen. It's different than what I expected, and it takes me a moment to understand why. The counters and cabinets are all low to the ground. I drag a chair over to one and sit in it. I can easily reach everything from this position and nod to myself. The place was clearly built with Ranger in mind or perhaps modified for him.

The kitchen is impeccably clean with a rack of drying dishes on the counter and only a coffee cup in the sink. Even his fridge is neat, his leftover dishes clearly labeled by date and contents.

Like the kitchen, the dining room is tidy. The round table has five chairs, and now I'm curious if Ranger's brothers often visit him. I imagine several of them playing cards around the table together and the thought makes me smile.

When I'm done in the kitchen and dining room, I wander into the living room. Above the dark leather couch is a large canvas print of a goose wrapping her wings around a yellow gosling with his eyes tightly closed.

The image makes me think of my mom. She left my father as his ideas became more radical. But she left us behind with him. She knew the path he was on and she saved herself.

I wonder why maternal instincts come so naturally to some women. Would I be one of them? Would I be the type of mom who would do whatever it takes to protect my babies, or would I abandon them when things got hard?

Shaking off the thoughts, I move to the bedroom. I don't know what I'm expecting but it's not this. Unlike the rest of the house that's harsh and masculine, this room is decorated in soft, pastel colors. The walls are slate gray while the white wrought-iron bed has a pale pink comforter on it. Next to the bed, there's a white table with a lamp already turned on, giving the room a soft glow.

The room is everything that Ranger is not. Soft, welcoming, and inviting. I don't understand why a man who would barely speak to me would go to all the trouble of creating such a cozy space.

"Maybe words are hard for you," I murmur as I run my fingers along the comforter. The plush material tells me it's expensive and the bed is decorated with pillows in matching colors. Each one is a different firmness, as if he wasn't quite sure what I would find comfortable.

I kick off my heels. I'm too tired from the long day of travel to be hungry, so I change into a white nightgown. It's a soft, cotton one with quarter-length sleeves and ruffles at the bottom. It's pretty but not sexy.

The wind rattles my windowpane with an eerie howl. I always have the worst trouble sleeping during snowstorms because they scare me. There's just something about waking up to find I've been snowed in that makes me feel claustrophobic.

Slipping between the cotton sheets, I let out a soft sigh. These are high-quality thread count, not the cheap stuff that I'm used to sleeping on. "You're a mystery, Ranger."

Ranger

A NOISE WAKES ME IN THE MIDDLE OF THE NIGHT, AND I sit up in bed. At first, I think it was the wind that startled me awake. But then I hear it again, the definite sound of someone moving about my house. It takes a moment for me to remember that I have a guest here. *Well, that's a hell of a way to describe her.*

I got married yesterday. I wanted to talk with her on the way home, but my muscles started tensing. I knew it would only be a matter of time before they spasmed, contorting my expression. I didn't want my wife seeing that so I hightailed it home as fast as I could and retreated to my bedroom.

I wait for the sound of the noise to stop and when it does, I lie back down in my bed. But then I hear a new noise through the paper-thin walls of the house. It's soft, like…aww, shit. She's crying.

There's a part of me that's tempted to let her be. After all, I don't want her seeing the spasticity.

Look at him. Here comes Quasimodo. Words from the high school girls echo in my head, but then I hear Tia sniff again. No matter how strange I might look right now, I can at least try to comfort her. I'm not entirely sure she'll accept my comfort but hell, I have to do something. I am her husband, and I did promise to take care of her.

Getting in my chair takes longer tonight because

the spasm is affecting my left arm, forcing it to contract against my body. I can't relax it or move it. My fingers are balled into a fist that I can't release.

I don't bother with a shirt. It'd be too difficult to put it on and besides, it's not like she's attracted to me if our earlier kiss was anything to go by. She didn't respond at all. She sat completely still during it.

As I wheel into the living room, I spot Tia on the couch. She's sitting on it with her knees pulled to her chest and a blanket draped around her shoulders. She sniffs after another loud gust shakes the house and says softly, "It's OK. You're OK."

I clear my throat, and she jumps. She probably didn't hear me enter the room over the sound of the storm. "The house is sturdy." My words come out as a growl because of the way my face is twisting.

She glances at me, frowning when she sees my face. I brace myself for her reaction, but she doesn't say anything about it. Instead, she scrubs a hand down her cheeks. Then she says in a voice so soft it's almost a whisper, "Sorry for waking you up. It's just a new place and I'm scared. Maybe you could not be mad at me for that."

I realize she must have assumed my look has to

do with her. "I'm not angry with you. My face does this. It's called a spasm."

She glances out the window, watching the storm. "It looks painful. Does it hurt?"

"Yep." Damn, she asks a lot of questions. I'm used to spending most of my time alone in the office or hanging out with my brothers whose ideas of deep conversations consist of whether the Packers will make it to the Super Bowl this year.

The wind rattles the back door, causing it to smack against the house and she startles. I recall what she said about being in a new place and feeling scared. The foster kid in me remembers what that's like. "What do you normally do when there's a storm?"

She pulls the blanket closer around her shoulders. It strikes me that she's trying to mimic the feeling of being held. "When I was little, I'd crawl into my big sister's bed. She always let me sleep beside her."

"Do you want to bunk with me?" The offer is out of my mouth before I can even think about it.

She chews her lower lip and studies me for a long moment. "You're a stranger."

"I'm your husband," I point out, wanting to put

her at ease. I don't know why I feel this way, why I want to help her. I'm not used to getting involved.

She frowns. "What does that mean to you?"

"It means you're safe with me." It's the best explanation I have. I haven't spent a whole lot of time thinking about what exactly marriage means.

My words seem to help her relax. There's something about her. An innocence I don't fully understand. Her background on the profile was scant. Just that she came from somewhere in the mountains. I probably should have asked a few questions when I met with Laney, the matchmaker, on video call. At that point, I was desperate to get the process over with. Now I'm wondering if that was a mistake. *Did Grandpa really know what he was doing or was this just an old man's last crazy idea?*

"You wouldn't mind?"

"Nope." This is all foreign territory to me. But I'm not about to leave her alone when she's feeling scared and vulnerable.

She hiccups. "Can we work on the one-word answers?"

"Sure."

Her mouth curves up in a grin, and I feel a rush of victory. I like her smile with that one snaggletooth. "Grab your pillow and follow me."

She pauses when she steps into the bedroom. I follow her gaze to see her staring at the large waterfall photograph above my bed. "You have a lot of nature photography."

"They're my own photos," I explain as I wheel to the bed. I scoot my pillows over, leaving her the side away from the window so she doesn't have to see the snowstorm that's still raging. "I win awards and stuff for them."

There's another grin and dammit, I could get addicted to making her smile. It's like watching a flower slowly open to the sun. "That's so cool. Where do you take them at?"

"On the farm. That waterfall is about thirty minutes from my place," I explain as I transfer myself from the chair to the bed. I rub my chest absently as I talk. That picture was from the last time Grandpa and I took that hike.

He'd told me Grandma had come to him in a dream and said that it was time to be with her again. In the moment, I'd brushed away his words as the musings of a lonely, old man. Now I'd give anything to go back and wrap my arm around his frail shoulders. I'd tell him I loved him one last time.

She joins me, moving slowly and hesitantly. She curls up on her side, facing me. "Is this OK?"

Her white nightgown is dipping low, letting me catch a glimpse of cleavage. I wonder what her tits look like then instantly dismiss the thought. I'm smart enough to know this marriage isn't going to include that.

"Yeah." I realize I gave her another one of the one-word answers she doesn't like and try again. "This is fine."

She pulls the covers up to her chin, pausing to burrow deeper into her pillow. The simple motion releases a lavender scent that has me wanting to lean close and sniff her skin. The idea is unsettling since I've never reacted to a woman this way. I've always known an intimate relationship wasn't in the cards for me and I've tried not to let myself want it. But lying next to her, I wish things could be different.

She yawns as the wind continues to batter the house. "It's our wedding night."

Images of how I'd like to spend it play in my mind and my cock lengthens in my cotton pants. I have to remind myself that the attraction isn't mutual.

She continues, "Do you think it's an omen that it's storming?"

I stare at the ceiling and recall the list of magazines my work has appeared in. It seems safer than focusing on the fact that I'm in bed with a beautiful woman beside me. "An omen?"

She's quiet for a long moment before she adds, "I mean, a prediction of what's to come. Like we'll have a bad marriage now?"

I can't help scoffing at the idea. "I don't believe in omens or signs. I think we'll have the kind of marriage that we decide to have and if we decide that it will be a good, happy one then that's what we'll find."

"I like that idea," she whispers as her eyelids drift closed.

I watch her sleep for the longest time, unable to tear my gaze away. She's a lot younger than me with an innocence that calls to me.

But I've seen the deepest, darkest parts of hell. I've been through the fires that shape you in irreparable ways. No matter what, I won't let my brokenness become hers. I'll fight every day for the rest of time to make sure that my darkness never extinguishes her light.

4
TIA

When I wake up, I can't remember where I am for one heart-pounding moment. Then the events of yesterday come flooding back. I'm a married woman, and I didn't marry just anyone. I married a quiet cowboy who is handsome. Kind too if last night was anything to go by.

I reach for his side of the bed to find it empty as the bathroom door opens. A rush of warm air greets me as Ranger rolls into the room. Since I've met him, I haven't seen anything that he can't do. It makes me wonder if he's a normal man down below. My cheeks heat at the thought.

I tried to hint around it last night by mentioning it was our wedding night. But Ranger never said anything that gave me a clear answer. Asking him outright seems mean. I don't want to make him feel bad if he can't do...*things*. More than that, I'm curious if intimacy is a possibility. Like a possibility after we've been married for a long time and are comfortable with each other.

He clears his throat. "I don't have time for breakfast, but help yourself to anything in the kitchen. I'll be back late."

"Wait." I sit up in the bed and fingercomb my hair. Something sparks in Ranger's gaze when I do this, but I can't decide what it is. "Where are you going?"

"To the office. I do the paperwork to keep the place running, remember?"

It was on his profile that he's the office manager for the ranch. But we never discussed what I'm supposed to do around the farm. I mean, the mail order bride service makes it clear that wives are supposed to assist their husbands in day-to-day tasks but there are no specifics. "What are my duties now that I'm here?"

He scratches the side of his freshly shaven jaw. His face is relaxed again today and so is his arm. Maybe the condition worsens only at night. "I hadn't thought that far ahead."

"Well, it's not like you need a housekeeper." I

can't help pointing that out. In the community, women are expected to keep the house and tend the babies. This place doesn't need much care and there are no babies.

"What skills do you have?"

I drop my eyes to the rumpled blankets, suddenly feeling stupid. Keeping house and cooking are the only things I know how to do. Prophet didn't believe that women needed a high school education and working outside the home was strictly forbidden.

"I was kind of sheltered," I force the words out. It's what Sarah told me to say if anyone asked why I seem different. She said it would be easier than explaining my background.

"If you come to the office with me, I reckon I can find something for you to do," he offers.

Ranger's office is in a workshop on the property. It's big with two chairs in front of his L-shaped desk and something he calls a dual monitor setup. I know how to use a computer thanks to Sarah. After I would read to the kids, she'd set me up on one and teach me the basics.

I survey the office, noting the dark oak flooring

and the wall of windows that allow him to overlook the rest of the snow-covered farm. It's a beautiful view but what I really love are the two giant bookcases in the corner. They're stocked with hundreds of books to the point that they're nearly overflowing. I long to reach out and run my fingertips across the spines but I don't dare.

"I can get you a desk in here soon," Ranger says, interrupting my curiosity about his books and what he likes to read.

"I'll be fine," I say as he pulls out a chair for me. He passes me something rectangular. A box that I recognize but I still freeze. Having so little access to technology means I'm not always sure what to do.

"For now, you can use the laptop," he explains.

He walks me through a few tasks that he calls data entry. Mainly, it's just putting numbers in the right columns. The work is easy but I'm careful to do it right.

I want to impress Ranger and show him that I'm dedicated to this marriage. Anything less and he might be tempted to send me back. My heart pounds at the thought and my stomach clenches. No matter what happens, I can't do that. I have to prove myself here.

"What are you doing?" I ask him after I've

finished the data entry. His face is scrunched in concentration. This is different than the way he looks when his face is spasming.

"I'll show you," he answers, gesturing for me to come to his side of the desk.

He turns his screen toward me when I join him, and I lean over his shoulder. I'm trying to see the number, and I catch a whiff of his cologne. It's spicy and masculine. I instantly like it simply because it's Ranger's scent.

"This is the payroll. I have to make sure all of our employees are paid, and this software helps me tally it up. But I still manually review everything myself," he explains as he clicks a button, and another column fills up.

"You're good at this," I compliment him. It's impressive the way he juggles all of these tasks for the ranch. He makes it seem easy.

"I have to be. The people that work on our ranch count on me."

For the next half hour, I watch him work. I ask question sometimes and he answers them. I like that he keeps explaining things to me without making me feel dumb or small. If anything, he seems excited by the possibility that I want to learn.

His phone rings, and he answers quickly. He

listens for a moment, pinching the bridge of his nose. Whoever is on the other end doesn't sound all that happy. He reassures Ethan that he's on the way then hangs up.

He frowns. "I have to go out for a bit. Do you want to give this a try?"

I nod, delighted that he's letting me help. "I'll do a good job."

Ranger doesn't return until late and when he does, he looks exhausted. But he gives me a small smile. Or he tries to. The muscles in his face have spasmed again and my heart hurts for him. I hate that he's in pain.

He quickly reviews the payroll I completed and nods. "You did really good."

I beam under the praise and wait while he shuts down the computer. When he's done, we leave for his house.

When we arrive, I take a shower while he prepares dinner. By the time, I emerge from the bathroom, he's already set the table. He pulls out a chair for me and I take the seat. He's been like that ever since I arrived, opening doors for me and pulling out chairs.

"So, you like to cook?" I ask as I twirl spaghetti noodles around my fork. Outside, the wind howls again. According to Ranger, it's usual to get this type of weather here in January though he assures me the snowstorm should let up in a day.

He takes a sip from his glass of water. The liquid dribbles down his chin, and he quickly swipes it away with a napkin. "Not particularly, but I like having someone to cook for."

For some reason, his answer warms me. I've never been around men that like to take care of their wives. Is he that kind of man?

He chews a bite of his food slowly. "Your profile said you lived in the mountains. Where about?"

I like that he's trying to get to know me. I just wish he wasn't asking about my past. I swallow a chunky tomato with a delicious garlic flavor. "Further down South."

He's not dissuaded by my vague answer. "Did you like it there?"

I'm not sure how to answer the question. I loved the mountains. The location was beautiful except for practically being held prisoner in the community by

Prophet. "Have you and your family lived on the farm your whole lives?"

Understanding crosses his features. He seems to sense that I need him to go first, to open up to me before I can tell him anything about my past. "My parents did. They couldn't have kids of their own, so they started adopting children from the foster system."

I've always been in awe of foster parents. To bring a child into your home and love them as fiercely as if they were your own, that takes a special kind of person. "All eight of you?"

A smile stretches across half of his face and amusement lights up his eyes. "Not all at once but yeah, they did. Mom used to joke that she collected odd things, and that's why she adopted us."

"She made you feel loved," I observe. It's obvious from the expression on his face that he was close to his foster parents. "What happened?"

"Cancer took her from us, and my dad went of a heart attack that night. We think it was a broken heart. They'd been inseparable their whole lives, and that left Grandpa with eight teenagers on his hands."

"It creates a hole in your heart," I answer and reach out across the table to take his hand. While I didn't lose my mom to cancer, I do understand loss.

He stares at our joined hands for a long moment before raising his gaze to mine. "I still have my brothers, but you seem alone."

I pull my hand back and give him a tight smile. "You cooked so it's only fair that I handle the dishes."

Standing, I gather the dishes and take them to the sink. But Ranger doesn't leave me to do them on my own. Instead he dries them, and we work together in a comfortable silence. Eventually, I'll have to figure out what to tell him. I just don't want him thinking that I'm an idiot that doesn't know anything. I definitely don't want him wondering if he should send me back.

When we're done with the task, he says, "You can bunk with me tonight."

The screen door bangs again, and I realize at his words that I'm dead on my feet. It's probably the stress of being in a new place and not sleeping last night.

I crawl into bed beside him. I'm determined to ask him more questions now that he's opening up to me. But first, I close my eyes for a little while.

A few minutes later, a masculine snore wakes me. I lift my head from Ranger's firm shoulder. Glancing at the alarm clock on the dresser, I see it's morning already.

The days start early here but at least the storm has passed. Funny that it didn't wake me once last night. When I'm next to my husband, I feel so safe. Like I'm cocooned from the world.

In the early morning light, I take the time to study my sleeping man. His chest is broad with patches of dark hair. Further down, his stomach is sculpted with a rippling six-pack. I have an overwhelming urge to touch him, and I trace my fingers over his warm skin gently. He's strong and firm, solid.

He makes a soft noise then blinks awake, eyeing me sleepily. "Good morning."

I continue running my fingers along his chest, curious about his body. I want to know everything about it, how he likes to be touched and what brings him pleasure. Even if we can't do everything, maybe we can touch in other ways.

"What do you want for breakfast?" I ask, trying not to focus on how nervous I feel. I've never done this before. Being promised to Prophet meant that I was carefully chaperoned and never allowed alone with a boy. Not that Ranger is a boy. No, he's all man, and there's a hunger in his eyes this morning.

He captures my wrist and growls, "Whatever you want to make is fine."

Then without another word, he pushes himself into a sitting position and transfers to his chair. He wheels into the bathroom and slams the door.

"That went well," I mutter to myself as the shower water starts.

5
RANGER

The moment I'm in the shower, my hand is wrapped around my aching cock. Only it's not my hand I'm thinking about. I'm imagining Tia's hand, stroking my stomach like she was in the bed.

Slowly, she slips it lower and lower until she's reaching into my pajama pants. She's looking up at me with her innocent doe eyes and those thick fuck-me lips as she squeezes me so tightly.

Something clicks softly but I ignore the sound, figuring it's the shower stool leg scraping against the tile.

She's pumping my shaft up and down, learning just how I like it. Her rhythm is relentless as she drives me over the edge until my come is shooting onto my stomach. Then she does the unexpected.

She drops her head and licks me, smacking her lips as she cleans every last drop of my seed from my body.

The dirty images have me erupting hot and sticky against the shower tile. But the moment it's over, white hot disappointment shoots through me. Because I wanted to share that with my wife. I want her to know my body and I ache to know hers.

Look at this! Krueger has a crush on me. I try to push back the memory but it's too late. I'd thought Lily and I were friends. I thought maybe she returned my feelings. That's why I gave her the stupid flowers. Then she told the whole school about it and that was when I realized that guys like me don't get to have a woman. We get to live out our days alone.

I finish my shower in cold water, hating the fact that I want my wife. I wish I'd found someone I felt no attraction to. But those big green eyes call to me, begging me to learn all of her secrets.

When I leave the bathroom, Tia has made us breakfast. We eat in silence, and I don't bother trying to start a conversation. The more distance I can keep between us, the better. She deserves more than I'll ever be able to give her.

She comes with me to the office. I'm tempted to tell her to stay home today but I don't want to see the look of disappointment on her face that I know would be there.

During the morning, I assign her more data entry. There are about a million things to track when you run a ranch. That's before you get into things like agricultural permits and USDA approval to sell our beef and poultry.

But Tia is a whiz at anything I throw her way and I'm impressed by her willingness to tackle new things. We make an amazing team together which is another reason I shouldn't fuck up and give into my attraction, no matter how hard it is to concentrate with her on the other side of my desk.

I need to order one and put her across the room. Even as I think the thought, I know it won't be far enough. She could be on the other side of the ranch and I'd still be thinking about her. Still be wanting to run my fingers through her silky hair and press my lips against her neck.

More than once though, I catch her gaze straying to the bookcases in the office. There's a gleam in her eye as she looks at them. She reminds me of a kid in a candy shop without a cent to her name.

When I catch her doing it again, I toss a pen on her side of the desk.

She glances at me and I nod toward the shelf.

"You're welcome to read whatever you want. There are books related to agriculture, small business practices, and nature photography. Afraid I'm not much of a fiction guy."

"I can read them?" She repeats.

"Read whatever sparks your interest."

I expect her to rush up and inspect the cases, but she keeps sitting there. She folds her hands in her lap and leans forward to ask quietly, "Is this a trap?"

For the life of me, I can't understand the question. "Why would it be?"

"You're telling me you won't be mad?" She chews her bottom lip, the same lip I want to kiss. "You promise?"

"Why on earth would I be mad at you for reading?" I can't imagine why it would matter. I certainly don't care what she reads.

She shrugs and drops her gaze to her lap. "Women aren't supposed to read where I come from."

Sensing the opening, I ask softly, "And why is that?"

"Prophet said no. Women are easily led astray and they don't know how to think for themselves. So, we can't have books or read them."

Holy hell, that's a lot of bullshit packed into just a

few sentences. "And remind me again. Who is Prophet?"

"Well, he was my future husband. I was going to be his sixth wife. But he wasn't..." Her voice drops to a whisper. "He wasn't a nice man like you are. My friend's husband said men on the outside are different...*kind*."

My Spidey senses are tingling and suddenly, her hesitancy to tell me about her past is making a lot of sense. And shit, she just said men on the outside. "Are you from a cult?"

She looks up then, frowning at me. "No, it was a church."

Instantly, I realize my mistake. I made her feel defensive. Softening my tone, I say, "Why don't you tell me about your church?"

By the time she's done talking to me an hour later, I'm fully convinced the place was a cult. Not that she seems to recognize this. But then again, she hasn't been out of it very long either.

I've also heard enough misogynistic statements to make me want to punch Prophet in the face. It's clear from the rules that they were created with the intention of keeping the women and children subservient to the men in the group.

I clear my throat. "Things are different now. You

can read books, watch TV, browse the internet. No one has permission over you."

She frowns like I just introduced a new concept to her and maybe I did. This is probably the first time in her life she's ever been given any type of freedom. The thought makes my stomach clench. How could they keep Tia with her bright mind trapped by all of these rules? Hell, they didn't let her finish school.

"Not even you?" She asks, studying me.

"Not even me. I'm your husband, not your warden," I reassure her. If I ever get a chance to meet her wacky ass father, we're going to have a man-to-man chat about how you raise daughters. I can't imagine bringing girls into this world and telling them they were second-best simply because of their gender.

The shy smile she gives me has me swearing that from this moment forward, I will make sure she has everything she could ever want. I'll encourage her to go after her dreams and stand in the shadows cheering her on the entire time.

I glance at the clock. "It's almost time for lunch. Take an early break and pick out something to read."

She nods and stands, moving to the bookcase. I admire the sway of her hips in that skirt as she walks. Suddenly, it occurs to me that I've never seen her in pants despite the fact that it's January. She's got to be cold and I'd bet anything there were rules against pants. If I ever get my hands on those fuckers, they're going to pay for the things they taught my wife.

She selects a book on agriculture that I've dog-eared and sits in the chair across from me. She tucks one leg under her as she starts reading, pronouncing the words under her breath.

I continue working, surprised by how much I like the sound of her quiet whispers. Finally, she gets to a word and stumbles. She tries again only to mispronounce it. She pulls her chair around my side of the desk. Placing the book in front of me, she points to the word, "What does it say?"

"Agroecology," I pronounce the word and sound it out for her. She might have made it to eighth grade, but I could tell from the way she was stumbling as she read that her education was substandard. I'd be willing to bet money that the school was somehow part of the cult she was in.

She repeats it twice and I coach her until she gets it right. She gives me a big smile when she does. "I did it."

That's when I lean in close to her, so close that

our breaths mingle. Her mossy gaze darkens, and I have the overwhelming urge to taste her sweet lips. But before I can, the sound of a throat clearing catches my attention. I pull away from her and straighten in my chair.

Looking up, I see Ethan in the doorway. "The door was open."

"It's fine," I gesture for him to come in. It's a good thing he arrived when he did. Because if he hadn't, I'd probably be kissing my wife right about now. "Ethan, this is Tia. My wife. This is my brother."

She gives him a radiant smile and damn, I want to clobber the bastard for being on the receiving end. I want to be the only one that ever gets her beautiful smiles, the only one she looks at. If that makes me a greedy, selfish bastard then so be it.

He gives her a polite nod but barely looks at her. Maybe he senses what I already know deep in my bones. There's something about this woman. *She's mine, and I won't share her with anyone.*

"What do you need?" I bark at my brother.

He gestures behind himself. "You wanted to go with me to check out the new tractor, but if you have something else to do…"

"No, let's do it," I say. Ethan is great at a lot of things. He gets shit done without batting an eye. But he's also become a hothead since the whole blow up with his wife and the slightest thing sets him off. He doesn't need to be in charge of negotiations with the seller.

"I'll wait out here." He moves to the door and pauses on his way out. He glances back at Tia. "Welcome to the family."

She thanks him then drops her attention back to the book.

How is it that I'm jealous of the lined pages that she runs her smooth hands across? I think again of the way she was touching my stomach this morning and I'm already hard again. Dammit, I have to get out of here. She's even more innocent than I suspected, and I need to go before I'm tempted to introduce her to every sinful fantasy I have.

6
TIA

He was going to kiss me...wasn't he? I don't understand my new husband at all. I thought he didn't like me. He pushed me away when I stroked his chest this morning. Then he went into the bathroom and touched himself.

I didn't mean to spy. I just knocked on the door and when he didn't answer, I stepped in. I worried maybe he'd fallen or something. But no, he was sitting in the shower and playing with his body.

Clearly, he can do some sexual things even though he hasn't tried to do anything with me. I can't help wondering why he hasn't. Does he think I'm plain or too big?

I glance down at my curvy hips. Prophet liked tiny women. Maybe Ranger does too. The thought makes my heart hurt. I don't want him to be anything like that man.

Before I can decide what to do, my phone rings with a call from Sarah. I promised her I'd check in when I got settled but I forgot.

"I'm good," I answer instead of greeting her. She worries about me and I feel terrible that I may have increased her anxiety. "I'm settling in."

She lets out a breath. "I was about to send out the National Guard."

I squeeze my eyes shut, surprised at how much I like to hear a familiar voice. She's the closest thing I have to any family now. "I know. I'm sorry."

She waits a beat. "I bet it's been hard on you."

"It's weird. He's a total stranger, and I'm married to him. I barely know anything about the man." Except that he's kind and likes photography.

"That will come in time," she reassures me.

"I'm not sure he likes me," I admit, a feeling of defeat settling over me. As silly as it sounds, I did come here with big dreams. I imagined falling instantly in love with my husband and having him feel the same way.

"Tell me about the last two days," she insists.

I summarize everything since the moment I stepped foot off the plane until now. By the time I'm done, I'm even more confused. Ranger is a mess of contradictions, and I'm not sure what to make of him.

"It'll get better. Give this thing time to work," Sarah says.

We chat for a few more minutes about how she's doing and what's happening at the library before she has to go. When the call is over, I feel lighter than I did before. Maybe in time this marriage will become a real one.

With that in mind, I get to work. I've only been here for two days but I'm getting a feel for the daily tasks. It's kind of fun to know that in some small way, I'm helping to keep this great, big ranch running.

I've been working for over an hour when a burly man I don't recognize stumbles into the office. The rage on his face has me wanting to hide under the desk. It was the same look my father would get before he decided that one of us was in need of a beating. Still, I manage to ask in a shaky voice, "What can I do for you?"

He slaps a piece of paper with a banking logo onto the desk and snarls, "Where is Ranger? Why the hell was my pay docked?"

I manage to swallow despite my dry throat. I

must have made a really big mistake with the software. "He's not here, but I did the payroll yesterday. If you'll let me take a look—"

He doesn't even let me finish my sentence. The vein in the middle of his forehead is bulging as he steps around the desk and grabs my arm hard enough to leave a bruise. "So, you're the dumb bitch who messed up?"

The word digs deep and reminds me of cowering under the kitchen table to avoid my father's wrath. I say quietly more to myself than him, "I'm not dumb."

"Fix it, moron!" Spittle flies from his mouth as he shouts at me.

My hands are shaky and I'm pretty sure I'm going to be sick. But before I can do anything, Ranger's voice is booming, "Unless you want to lose that hand, let go of her. Right. Now."

The man releases me and spins around to glare at Ranger. "The dumb bitch messed up my pay this week."

I've never seen Ranger look angry. But in this moment, he looks downright menacing and I worry he's mad at me.

When he speaks, it's obvious that I'm not the target of his rage. "I don't give a damn if all you got was a dollar, Declan. You don't put your fuckin' hands on my wife."

A little bit of color drains from Declan's face. I guess he didn't realize he was manhandling Ranger's wife. Still, he grabs for the sheet of paper that I realize now is some type of bank statement. "You fix this."

A muscle tics in Ranger's jaw. "It'll be fixed by the end of the day. But you're no longer employed by the Scott Ranch. Now get the hell off my property before I call the sheriff."

"I don't need this shitty job anyway. A lot of places around here need ranch hands." Declan says, stomping from the office. He slams the door on the way out, the glass rattling.

The moment I know he's out of the building, I sink into a chair. I clasp my shaking hands together tightly, trying not to imagine what will happen when he sends me back. I'll call Sarah. Maybe she can help me again. "I'm sorry."

His fingers are against my chin, tilting up my face. Concern is etched in his eyes. "Are you hurt?"

My arm is a little sore but it's nothing worth making a fuss over. "I didn't mean to mess up the payroll. He was just in here all of the sudden and so loud."

He studies me for a long moment before saying, "I'm the king of this place. Do you know what that means?"

"No." The single word is quiet, and my heart is pounding.

"It means you are my queen. You cower before no one and you bow to no one. Every person in this place owes you nothing less than their complete respect and honor. If anyone treats you like he did, you let me know. I will never tolerate *anyone* disrespecting my woman."

"But it was my mistake."

He shakes his head. "I checked over the work. I should have caught it, and even if you were to blame, he can't just walk in here and manhandle you. No man has the right to put their hands on you."

"You defended me," I whisper the words. I've never had anyone defend me. I mean, my older sisters always defended me against my father's rage, usually paying the price for their defiance. But I've never had a man stand up for me.

He cups my jaw, running his calloused thumb along my face. "I'll always defend you, my queen."

I like the endearment, the idea that I belong to him. I lick my bottom lip before whispering the one thing I've wanted to say since this morning, "Then kiss me."

His mouth curves up in a grin before he threads his fingers through my hair and angles my head. He brushes his lips over mine gently, pressing little kisses to the corners of my lips.

I melt into his embrace, tugging on his shirt to pull him closer. I want him so close that our bodies are fused together. I want to feel him against me, skin-to-skin. It's a heady feeling, one I've never experienced.

His tongue sweeps into my mouth and I can't help whimpering. Despite his harsh looks and commanding presence, everything about Ranger is gentle in this moment. From the way he's cradling my head to the way his tongue strokes across mine. It's as if I'm precious to him, someone that he treasures.

Ranger pulls away, and I blink. My lips feel swollen and all I want is to climb into his lap and do that again for a few hours. Is this why people like kissing?

He scowls and turns his attention to the doorway. There's another man standing there, looking just as angry as Declan did. But I don't feel afraid now. Not with Ranger right beside me. He's made it clear he's my protector.

"I'm installing a fuckin' lock on that door," Ranger growls under his breath.

The man stomps into the room. "You fired my man because he complained about a paycheck error? That was a dick move, Range."

"Tia, this is my brother, Logan. He's in charge of managing the ranch hands."

"It's good to have you here, Tia." Logan tips his hat toward me before turning his attention back to my husband. My husband who just gave me the best kiss of my life. "Declan is one of my hardest workers. I can't keep up with the workload if you fire my best men."

Ranger glares at him. "Declan put his hands on my wife."

Logan rears back as if he's been slapped. He glances at me. "That is not how we allow our ranch hands to behave. It'll never happen again. You have my word."

I'm not sure what to say or even really why Logan is apologizing. He wasn't the one who grabbed me. That was all Declan. It's odd, the way these brothers live. I can't quite figure them out.

"You'd better pray it never happens again. I'll fire

your entire crew for so much as looking at her wrong," Ranger warns.

Logan nods, seeming to accept the reprimand. "They'll be informed. Nothing like this will ever go down again."

My husband still doesn't look appeased. "See that it doesn't. Now, get your ass out of here before I fire you too."

His brother chuckles at the joke and looks to me one final time. "Truly am sorry, Tia."

Then he's gone out the door and I'm left to decipher what just happened. "He didn't owe me an apology."

"The hell he didn't. Those are his men. The choices they make are a reflection not just on him but on the whole Scott Ranch. The hands we hire know this and we hold them to a high standard."

"I think I like cowboys," I say, realizing how safe I feel here. Declan scared me, true. But the quick response of Ranger and Logan has me realizing that Sarah's husband was right. Men on the outside are different. They didn't turn a blind eye or say it was his right. Instead, they were quick to side with me.

Ranger growls at my statement.

"I like a cowboy," I correct, my cheeks growing hot.

"That's the right answer, my queen," he says, brushing a lock of hair out of my face. He lets his fingertips trail across my cheek again, something sparking in his gaze. I don't know what changed between now and this morning, but whatever it is, I'm grateful for it.

He grins at me, mischief in his expression. He looks like a little boy with a slingshot when his teacher's back is turned. "I have an idea. Let's close up early and go on an adventure."

"What kind of adventure?" I ask, already knowing that I'm going to follow him wherever he goes. I think I might just be falling in love with my new husband.

7
TIA

"You'll have to come with me to see," Ranger teases. "Otherwise, you might miss out."

My stomach growls. "Does the adventure include lunch?"

He winks, and I'm surprised by how much I like this fun, playful side of my husband. I didn't even know it existed until this afternoon. "You bet."

It only takes us a few minutes to end our workday and I grab my coat from the rack. It was a thrift store find that isn't all that warm.

He scowls when he realizes it's threadbare and insists I take his. I start to protest but the look in his eyes tells me he's not taking no for an answer. Since I've arrived, Ranger has prepared a room for me, cooked for me, comforted me when I was scared, and even defended me. Oh, and he kissed me. Like really kissed me.

He opens the door to his truck, warning me to watch for the ice on the step bar.

"Are you going to give me a hint where we're going?" I ask once we're settled in his truck and on the road.

I notice the way his large hands swiftly work the controls. There are more levers than I've ever seen in a vehicle. But he handles them all with ease. I wonder if I asked if he'd teach me to drive. It's the one skill I've always wanted to master.

"Lunch first then the adventure," he promises.

For lunch, he takes me to the local diner where he orders two burgers all the way and milkshakes. I keep smiling so much that it feels like my face is going to crack. Having Ranger defend me today put some of my fears to rest. We're still getting to know each other and sure there will still be a lot of difficult moments ahead for us, but he likes me.

"What do you want to do?" He asks when the waitress has delivered the food, including a large platter of chili cheese fries for us to split.

I pick up a fry and pop it in my mouth, groaning at the taste. It's the perfect amount of spicy chili and gooey cheese to satisfy my tastebuds. I could gorge myself on this. "Go on an adventure with you."

He takes a bite of his burger and chews. "No, what do you want to do with your life? I don't imagine that you thought you'd spend your days working on a ranch."

"I like it there," I answer sincerely. There's something about the ranch. It feels like home in a way nothing else ever has. The only thing that would make it perfect would be if my sisters were here too, but that's not going to happen. I'll always ache for them, for my sister that went missing and my sister that was too far gone to get herself out.

He reaches across the table and takes my hand. "What's upsetting you?"

"I miss my family," I say before I tell him about my sisters. I tell him about how much I love them, about the funny things we did together as kids, and the battered women they became. "I'm glad I didn't follow in their footsteps. But I feel guilty for getting out. For being here with you."

"Maybe one day their stories will be different. People can change," he reassures me as he passes me a napkin. "*Dum spiro spero.* It means while I breathe, I hope."

I squeeze his strong fingers before I blot my face.

I didn't even realize I'd started crying. "I like that phrase."

"It's Latin. My mom loved the language. She was always trying to get one of her boys to learn it but none of us took to it," he says before launching into stories from his own childhood. It's clear from the funny tales he's sharing that he's trying to lift my mood. He manages to make me laugh and by the time we leave the diner, I'm feeling strong and hopeful again.

The drive to Asheville doesn't take any time at all. Mainly because Ranger puts on something called an MP3 player and plays his music. He explains that I have a few decades of good tunes to catch up on.

When he pulls into the parking lot of our destination, I can't help smiling up at the big store with the book logo. "We're going here?" I don't hide the squeal of excitement in my voice.

He flashes me a grin. "Yep, it's time to start building your own personal library."

"Really? I can get books?" I'm practically vibrating with anticipation as we enter the store. The place even smells amazing, like coffee, ink, and pages. It's the most wonderful smell on earth.

The store is easily twice the size of the local

library where I would hang out with Sarah. I know she'd love it here.

"I want to take one of those self-photos people do," I tell Ranger when we're inside as I pull out my cellphone. "My friend will love this."

"They're called selfies," Ranger clarifies and waits for me to take one.

I hesitate after I've sent the photo and look up at my husband. "Do you want to take one together?" I've seen them on the social media apps. Husbands and wives taking selfies together. They always look so cute.

He nods and when I lean close to him, he presses a kiss to my cheek right as I snap the photo. I smile at the image. That one I won't share with Sarah. I won't share it with anyone. It's too special.

"Come on. Let's go browse. You can get as many books as you can fit into the truck."

I laugh. "I will hold you to that."

Four hours later and the truck is loaded down with hundreds of books. Ranger paid a couple of young boys to follow us around, carrying my books.

Now they've finished loading up the truck and he tips them generously again.

I lean into the seat when we're in the truck. "That was the most fun I've ever had."

He pauses before he starts the ignition and turns to me, a serious look on his face. "I wanted to show you that I'm never going to stand in your way. Whatever you want to do in your life, I want to support that. I'll support *you*."

His words warm me. Is this what makes a marriage a good one? I hope so because it definitely feels like it. "I'll support you too. I want us to have a good marriage, like you said."

"We will," he promises as he starts the truck.

When we get home, Ranger and I spend over an hour unloading my books. We put them in my bedroom where bookshelves have materialized. I think Ranger called one of his brothers and had them added to the house.

"How should I arrange them?" I ask as I bend to separate the books into piles. So far, I've settled for sorting them between fiction and non-fiction. There are a few mixed in here that I don't remember getting, but I did see Ranger adding a few to my collection. These must be from him.

"Organize them however you want," his voice has

a funny note and I stand up right, glancing at his face. There's longing on it again. The way there was this morning when I was touching him.

I start to bring it up, what I saw him doing in the bathroom, then decide against it. Maybe that's all he can do. Maybe he can't make love and I'd never want to embarrass him over it.

We continue to work together, though we're doing it in silence. I don't understand this sudden tension between us. We've been getting along so well but now, I don't know what to say to him or why I feel awkward again.

I decide on my book arrangement, separating non-fiction and fiction on different bookcases. But each collection is still sorted the same way, by the author's last name. It'll have to work for now until I can get more specific.

I think Ranger bought me books on just about every subject in the store. I love that he seems to understand how hungry it makes you for knowledge when you've been denied it your whole life.

When I finish arranging everything, it's late and my body is aching from the endless bending and stooping. I can't wait to spend all of my time reading.

"It seems like a dream," I tell Ranger as I run my

fingers across the spines of the books. I don't think I'll ever get tired of the way they feel.

He murmurs something under his breath. It sounds like he called me his dream, but I know that can't be right. I'm just imagining what I want him to say. I manage an embarrassed chuckle and keep my eyes on the floor, "I should probably take a shower."

I move to pass by his chair, but he grabs my wrist. When I glance at him, he tugs me onto his lap. He presses his lips against mine in a slow, hungry kiss and in this moment, I know I didn't imagine it. He called me his dream a moment ago.

I put my hands on his shoulders and press my chest against his, the way I wanted to earlier. Something about it feels so right and I can't stop myself from rubbing up against him. Even if we never do it completely, this feels pretty amazing to me.

His big hand finds the hem of my t-shirt and he slips beneath it. He strokes my stomach with his thumb while he continues to plunder my mouth with his tongue. The dual sensations have something starting in my thighs. I can't describe it. I don't know how to, all I know is I can't get comfortable.

When I start wiggling, I feel Ranger's body beneath me. A rush of desire runs through me even as I blush.

He breaks the kiss and squeezes a handful of my generous hip. "You can't keep moving like that or this show will be over before the opening credits."

I'm not sure what he means, and I can't say that I care. I just want to slide my body against his. Surely, we can do that much, right?

Taking a deep breath for courage, I put a hand on his face and cup it. "Are we going to try to do what husbands and wives do?"

8
RANGER

"Are we going to do what husbands and wives do?" I ask and frown. I shouldn't tease her, but I love that innocent blush on her face. The one that tells me this is her first time just like it's mine.

She nods, her gaze dark with desire. "I'd never make you feel bad…if you couldn't do it because you're…"

We've never had a conversation about the chair or why I'm in it. But those aren't things I want to discuss. Not with her on my lap and wiggling against my hard-on every few seconds. I don't think she even realizes she's doing it.

"Paraplegic," I supply the word. I've been like this since the day I was born so to me, the chair is just an extension of my body. The same way most able-bodied people don't think about their legs, I don't think about my chair.

She repeats the words softly, giving me a solemn nod. I can see in her face how badly she wants to get this right. The way she doesn't want to hurt my feelings and it warms something in me that she cares so much.

"I can have sex," I assure her. Well, that much is a guess since I've never gotten anything but solo action. Still given the fact that I can come, I don't see why I wouldn't be able to with a partner. I wouldn't be coming with just anyone either. It'd be with my wife.

Her expression is a mix of hopeful and nervous. Just like that, I know she needs me to take the lead on this. But that doesn't bother me. I'll always go first and show her the path when she needs it and I'll cheer her on when she doesn't need my guidance.

I can't help giving her a wicked grin. "It's time for bed."

Tia

My stomach flips when Ranger growls at me. The rough, commanding note in his tone has that pain between my legs increasing. Something tells me that his body can make it go away.

Ranger spins the chair around and wheels out of my bedroom. I try to leave his lap since I can walk, but he only squeezes me tighter. I like the way his arms are locked around me, as if he can't stand the idea of letting me go for even a minute.

When we're in his room, he flicks on the light switch before setting me gently on the bed.

"You are so beautiful," he murmurs. I rarely feel beautiful but with the way he's staring down at me, I can't help but believe it. There's so much intensity and longing on his face. So many emotions flickering across it.

"And you're handsome," I tell him.

His expression lights up and I realize that he must have needed the reassurance as much as me. I'd never considered how a man wants to know he's attractive just as much as a woman. I guess wanting to be desired is a universal feeling.

He joins me on the bed. Despite the fact that he can't move his lower half, his movements are still quick and fluid. I can't help but admire a man who has seen so much and hasn't let anything slow him down. He's just as determined to build a good life for himself and I've never seen him once complain about the hand he was dealt.

"I'm glad you're here," he whispers quietly right before he captures my lips in a soft kiss. If I thought kissing him before was fun, it's nothing compared to how wonderful it feels when I'm lying here next to him.

The fire between my thighs is back again and I clench my legs together, trying to get relief from the pain I've never felt before.

Ranger's lips slide lower, down the side of my neck and to the collar of my shirt. He kisses the exposed skin there, leaving what feels like glowing coals behind. My body is too hot, and my heart is racing.

His earlier words register. *I'm glad I'm here too.*

"Take off your shirt for me," he commands.

I hesitate for a second. I've never been naked in front of a man. But more than that, Ranger and I are very different. He's all hard muscle and lean lines. I'm big and fluffy and soft. I've seen the pictures of what women in his world are supposed to look like, and I don't fit the standard.

He cups my face. "I chose you, Tia. Before I saw

your face or knew what you would look like, I wanted *you*."

My heart sinks at his use of my new name. There's still so much he doesn't know about me. So many things that I want to tell him. How is it that after a lifetime of feeling as if I had to hide my heart, I want to open it and show this man everything?

"Rebecca," I say the word softly. "My real name is Rebecca. Prophet picked the name because it means to bind. He determined when I was just a baby that I would be bound to him."

He studies my face. "But you chose a new name."

"Tia means happiness and joy. I want those things," I explain. I think I've found them here with Ranger but I'm not about to tell him that. I love him so much that it would break my heart if he didn't feel the same way. The realization knocks the breath from my lungs. I'm in love with Ranger. He's my home now, my refuge and my defender.

His eyes are smiling at me when he speaks, "You recreated yourself. Like a butterfly, you broke through the darkness to discover your wings."

The compassion in his gaze has me sitting up long enough to peel my t-shirt from my body. He watches me with a hooded gaze, running his tongue along his bottom lip like he just spied a treat he can't wait to eat. Something about that look makes my stomach flip. But not in a scared or nervous way. No, this is something else. Something that makes me desire him even more.

He reaches for the clasp on my plain, white bra. "Can I?"

I nod, my breaths shallow as he unclasps it and gently tugs the straps down. Then he pulls off the cups, and he stares at my bare breasts for a moment before he says, "So pretty."

He ducks his head and presses his mouth to the swell of my breast, placing feather-light kisses everywhere. His tongue finds my nipple and swirls around the little nub.

I groan his name as I lean back against the pillows. I don't know why I like it so much, but his tongue and lips are doing something funny to my breasts. He's making them feel heavy and tingly.

He sucks one of my nipples into his mouth in a motion that creates a tugging down below. Just when I think I can't take it anymore, he moves to my other breast and lavishes his attention on it. He's making tiny grunts and groans as he feasts on my body.

But whatever he's doing, it's connected to my thighs. It has to be because there's a growing need down there. I wish I could explain it, but I only know that I need something. Something I think Ranger will be able to give me.

I thread my fingers through his thick hair and tug lightly.

He lifts his head, and his eyes are different now. They're completely black and yet so full of light and happiness. His voice is dark and gritty in a way it normally isn't. "What's wrong?"

"I'm hurting," I reach for the words, hoping they're the right ones. I wish I could explain all of this, that he could understand.

His gaze searches mine. "Where?"

My cheeks heat. "Down."

He frowns for a moment before understanding flickers across his features. "Does it feel achy, tight, or tingly?"

I nod, relieved that he seems to grasp what I'm going through.

His voice is quiet when he speaks and his words are measured, as though he's choosing them carefully. "Tia, how much were you told about sex?"

"I know what goes where," I say, suddenly defensive. I did manage to cobble that much together. Sex was something shameful and good girls weren't supposed to talk about it.

"There's a hell of a lot more to it than that," he mutters before letting out a soft sigh. "What you're feeling is likely arousal. Your body is preparing you for sex. You're probably wet and swollen too."

I'm silent for a beat, letting this new knowledge sink in. "Is that bad?"

"Your body is functioning in the way it's designed to. It's completely normal. I can make that ache go away. But only if you want me to."

I don't even have to think about my answer. I nod quickly and wait to see what he'll do. I don't know what comes next. All I know is that since I've arrived, Ranger has done everything possible to take care of me.

He leans forward and presses gentle kisses to my bare stomach while running his thumb along my stretch marks. It doesn't seem like he's repulsed by the curvy rolls of fluff. If anything, he's touching them reverently, like he's worshipping my body. I've never felt prettier.

He continues lower until he reaches the waistband of my skirt. He glances up at me as if he's seeking permission. When I give him a nod, he gently tugs on the side zipper.

I shimmy out of the material and he tosses it onto the floor. Suddenly, I'm in front of Ranger in just my underwear. My wet underwear. Wow, he was right. It is wet. I'm wet down there. The knowledge has me clamping my thighs together so he can't see it.

He puts a hand on my stomach and instantly, I calm under his touch. "Completely normal, remember?"

I manage a nod, surprised that he knew I needed the reminder. He reads my moods, sensing what I need and giving it to me without holding anything back. Ranger is more than just strong and kind. He's generous too.

"Spread your legs for me," he says.

I hesitate. What if he doesn't like it? What if he's wrong and I am weird? What if he regrets marrying me and thinks—?

"Tia," he calls my name sharply.

It's enough to pull me from my anxious thoughts as I focus on him.

He touches himself, grinding his hand against the center of his blue jeans. "I'm aching right now, just like you are. You have no idea what it's doing to me, to smell your sweet arousal. Spread your legs, and I'll help both of us."

I do as he says this time. I didn't realize he was feeling the same things I was and for some reason that eases my anxiety.

When I spread my legs, he reaches for my panties. He pulls them from my body and presses a soft kiss to the inside of my ankle and works his way up my leg. He alternates between kisses and licks. His stubble scratches my skin, creating a delicious contrast to the softness.

Then he reaches the place between my thighs and to my surprise, he places a kiss there. It's tender, more like a gentle caress. He looks up at me then. "Again?"

I give him a nod, and he presses more kisses to different spots until everything starts to blend together in this delicious haze of pleasure. That's when he does the last thing I ever expected. He licks me, but the weird thing is it feels good. So, so good.

When I whimper, he licks me again. He traces my body with his tongue for what feels like hours then suddenly, he's sucking on me. Just like he did with my breasts. Only the difference is that my body starts to tingle all over, and I begin moving my hips against his face.

Without warning, there's a blinding light and all of my muscles go tight. I can't move or breathe. There's only the sensation of his lips against me, still suckling between my thighs.

"Ranger," I call his name in a whisper. I'm not

entirely sure what's happening but it feels amazing and great and special all at the same time.

He presses a gentle kiss to my mound as the sensations begin to fade. All I'm left with is a rush of contentment and warmth. I definitely never heard any of the women I know talk about *that*. "What happened?"

Ranger scoots up on the bed and kisses the shell of my ear. "You probably had your first orgasm. It's why sex feels good."

I turn in his arms, fighting a yawn. He said he was aching too. "I want to touch you. I don't know how to make you feel good, but I want to try."

A small smile curves those full lips of his. "Tomorrow. You're exhausted."

I lose the battle with the next yawn as I realize I'm naked while he's fully clothed. It seems wrong that he just gave me something so wonderful and he's still aching. "It's not fair."

"Trust me, butterfly. There's still so much we'll learn together." He presses a kiss to my forehead. "Sleep now. I plan to wear you out tomorrow."

9
RANGER

I WAKE TO THE SCENT OF LAVENDER AND A TICKLE IN my nose. That's when I realize that Tia's hair is on my face. I brush it away, unable to help the smile that comes when I think about last night.

Damn, I loved discovering what she tasted like. I wanted to take her so badly after that. I wanted to hear her whisper my name in the throes of ecstasy again and again. But realizing she had next to nothing in the way of a sex education made me slow down.

We might both be virgins, but I know a hell of a lot more than her. When she talked, it was obvious she didn't even have the vocabulary to describe what she was feeling. It makes me angry that she was denied a basic education about her body. I'll never understand religions that keep women in the dark about their bodies or sex.

I want Tia to know her body, to understand how it works. I want her to be able to describe what she's feeling and know what she likes. I want her to be empowered to make sexual choices that are right for her.

She stirs beside me and I pull her even closer. When I look at her, I see all the dreams I always wanted. The things that I've convinced myself were never a possibility. But what if I was wrong? What if everything I wanted could happen, a happy wife and children of my own?

She blinks awake slowly, smiling up at me. I love that sleepy look in her eyes and the way her cheeks are flushed. Every part of me wants to make love to her right now but that's not what she needs just yet. "You want to try some of my world-famous pancakes?"

"Who could turn down world-famous pancakes?" She teases.

After a leisurely breakfast where I feed her bites of pancakes while she sits next to me, she reaches to gather the plates. "We're going to be late."

For once in my life, I don't give a damn about being the first one at work on the ranch. I don't even care if I go in at all today. There's only one thing I plan to do.

I reach for her hand, stilling her motions. "Take a shower with me."

She drops her gaze. "We can't do that together."

"We're married," I remind her. As soon as I say the words, they sting. She told me last night that Tia isn't her real name. I didn't realize until after she'd fallen asleep what that means. We're not legally married. "Besides, good things happen when you get naked around me."

She grins at that and her smile fills me with contentment. I plan to keep her satisfied in and out of the bedroom for the rest of time.

In the shower, I guide her to the bench while I sit on the stool across from her. "Put your feet on my knees."

She squirms, clearly uncomfortable with the request that will open her entire body to my view. I hate that she feels as if she has to hide any part of herself from me. "Tia, I'm your husband. There's no shame between us."

We may not be legally married just yet. But I am her husband. I will always belong to her, just like she'll always belong to me. "You need to understand your body. This is about a hell of a lot more than sex. What if you need medical attention one day? You need to be able to tell a doctor what's going on."

It takes a bit more coaxing, but she does as I ask. Then I'm touching her, giving her the words to describe the parts of her anatomy. I choose the proper terms, avoiding anything slang. Right now, I'm thankful that I brushed up on how a woman's body works after I signed that marriage contract.

The entire time we're talking, I keep pausing to squeeze my hard cock. It's downright painful to be having this conversation. My body is screaming at me to plow into her, to claim my wife. My mind is saying that she'll remember our first time together for the rest of her life and I need to make it good for her.

When I'm done, she's glistening, and the smell of her arousal is heavy in the steamy shower air. Even though it wasn't my intention, talking about her body excited her. She's horny now and damn, so am I.

She licks her lips and drops her gaze to where I'm still strangling my cock. He twitches. "Tell me how your body works now."

Then she does what I didn't expect. She reaches

out and touches me, putting her hand over mine. There's curiosity and fascination on her face.

Reaching down, I lift my legs and spread them apart. "Touch yourself. Get your fingers nice and soaked."

She does that, and I show her how to glide her hands all over me. Her sticky juices coat me as her fingers trace my body. I never thought I could be this aroused, and I'm counting backwards to keep from coming in her hand. When I can't take it anymore, I say, "I need to come inside of you."

Excitement flickers in her gaze. "Can we do that now?"

I glance around the hard, unforgiving surfaces of the shower. The logistics will be a little easier in the bed. "In the bedroom."

She cuts off the shower water and I drape a hot towel around her shoulders. I love taking care of my woman. Hell, I love my woman. The knowledge stops me in my tracks, and I pause between the bathroom and the bedroom. I love my wife.

She glances at me over her shoulder. Her expression is shy and uncertain again. "Did you change your mind?"

"I'd never change my mind about wanting you,"

my voice comes out gruffer than I intend as I wonder if she'd ever feel the same way about me. It seems like a long shot but maybe one day, our marriage could be more than just an escape from her horrible home life.

Tia

SOMETHING FLICKERS ACROSS RANGER'S EXPRESSION. I don't know what it is but for a moment, he almost looks sad. I want to reach out and touch his face, to reassure him that whatever is wrong, we can figure it out together. "Did you change your mind?"

He glances toward the bed, heat flaring in his gaze. "I'd never change my mind about wanting you."

Despite how hard Ranger is, he still takes the time to lick me again. He called it oral sex when he was describing it in the shower. I call it heaven. Nothing feels better than his mouth and tongue on me. This time, it's even more satisfying because he works a finger inside of my body. I understand what he's doing, the way he's mimicking what he's about to do to me.

Something about his frank explanations in the shower helped me to relax about sex. It doesn't seem quite so big and overwhelming now that I understand how our bodies will work together.

My channel tightens around his finger as a wave of pleasure sweeps over me. This one is different than last night. It's bigger and deeper but Ranger is with me, pressing kisses all over my body and murmuring things under his breath. I think maybe he says he loves me, but I decide I'm imagining that. It was only the orgasm talking.

As I float back down to earth, I press a kiss to my husband's neck. "Now I get to make you…come?" I think that's the word he used earlier. There were a lot of things to remember all at once.

He gasps and angles his head, so I continue nuzzling his neck. He likes it when I suck on his skin right here. I make a note of that, so I can do it again in the future. I want to have a lot of sex with my handsome husband.

"Get on top of me."

I force myself to stop kissing him. I really like the taste of his skin. "How?"

He uses his hands to guide me over his body. I hover above him, too afraid to sit down. I'm certain I'll crush him. His body is bigger than mine, that's true. But I'm not exactly delicate. "I think maybe we should try this another way."

"You can do this, butterfly," he croons with a hand on my back. The gentle pressure he's applying makes me wish he'd slide his hand lower and squeeze my bottom.

"I'm too big," I admit, embarrassed that I have to say it.

A grin spreads across his face as he uses his other hand to grip my hip. "You're amazing. I love these curves. I plan to worship them every day."

My thighs ache from the weight of supporting myself. "Are you sure?"

His voice is rough and gritty when he speaks, "On my cock is where you belong. Now take your place, my queen."

At his words, I start to slide onto him. I go slow so I don't hurt him. He warned me in the shower that the first time might hurt but I'm so wet and so ready for this that all I feel is a minor pinch. It's the quickest bite of pain then it's over. Now all that's left is pleasure. This is even better than when he had his fingers in my body.

I can't help the triumphant grin that spreads across my face when I see Ranger's expression. He looks just as blissful as I feel when he starts licking me. Maybe this is the same concept for him.

I brace my hands on his chest and lean forward to press a kiss to his pecs. His rough hair tickles my face. "Is this it?"

"Try to move in a way that feels good to you," his voice is small and strangled.

"What about you?" He's already made me feel good twice now. I want to do that for him. "I don't know what I'm doing. Maybe this was dumb."

Suddenly, I feel like a failure. Other wives probably know how to do this. They can probably do it easily.

I try to lift off of him, but Ranger's hands squeeze my hips, keeping me in place. "This is my first time, too. We're figuring it out together. Now, move your hips. Use my body to find your pleasure. Mine will follow yours."

It takes me trying several different motions but then I find one that has me whimpering at the same time that he groans.

"That's right," he murmurs. "Ride your man."

The wet slap of our skin fills the room as I discover the rhythm that makes both of us happy. Even though he's not moving, Ranger is still panting.

There's a wild look in his eyes and he's biting down on his lip.

I want to tell him that being with him is special to me and that I love him. But I'm not sure he'd say it back and my heart can't take that right now. Instead I close my eyes, so he won't see my feelings. I focus on rocking against him, the pleasure of our bodies connecting.

"I'm about to come," he warns then his rough fingers are against my clit.

Between the feeling of being filled completely by my husband and his fingers pressing against that magical spot, I come. My body clenches around him and seconds later, he's spurting inside of me. He's filling me with his seed.

As I collapse against him, I can't help but wonder if we'll get pregnant. I'd love to carry his children someday. I'd like to see Ranger holding our babies and singing them to sleep at night. Something tells me he'd be good at that.

I don't know how long we stay wrapped up in each other but eventually I roll off of his body and onto the sheets.

He reaches for my face, cupping it. "That was amazing."

I can't help but smile at his compliment. "I was so worried I was going to hurt you." We stay snuggled together for long moments, not saying a word. I'm thinking about the future and what it might look like. I see Ranger with little boys, teaching them how to build forts and showing them how to care for the ranch.

The more I think about it, the more I realize there's something I want to know. Clearing my throat, I say, "I need to ask you something, and I don't want to hurt your feelings."

He nods at me to continue.

I take a moment to gather my thoughts before I say, "I know that what we did just now means there's a chance of pregnancy."

Longing flickers across his face before he quickly hides it. He keeps his tone gentle as he asks, "Are you worried I'd ask you to carry a child you don't want?"

"No, that's not it. It's just you said you're paraplegic. Is that…genetic? Would our baby be not able to move?" I love Ranger just as he is. I wouldn't change a thing about him. But I imagine that his life is much harder than it has to be since he can't move.

He untangles his body from me and sits up in the bed. His tone is flat when he says, "No, it's not genetic."

I wait for him to tell me more, but he doesn't. He

reaches for his boxers and slips into them before getting into his chair. He wheels toward the walk-in closet.

"Would you talk to me?" I ask, hating that I've clearly poked at a wound I don't understand.

He pauses but he won't look at me. Then in a voice that breaks with emotion, he says, "I killed my mom. That's why I'm like this."

10
TIA

I don't think for a moment that he did that. But I stay completely still and silently will him to open up to me.

"It was a complicated delivery. I made it, but she didn't. My brain was deprived of oxygen and well, that's how you end up in a chair." His hands are clenched into fists and he stares down at them. "It's my punishment for taking her life."

I can't help it then. I move from the bed and kneel in front of Ranger's chair. Putting my hand on his face, I whisper, "You didn't do anything wrong."

When he looks up at me, there's so much heartache in his gaze. "I'm here, and she's not. My own dad didn't want me after that. That's why I was in the system."

My heart breaks for a little boy who had to grow up carrying such a heavy burden. "I think she's looking down at you from Heaven. She's so proud of her boy and all he's accomplished."

I don't know what else to do, so I give him a hug. He clings to me like I'm a life preserver, and I wish I could take this pain from him.

It's on the tip of my tongue to tell him I love him when there's a knock at the front door. It's loud and insistent. "Come on, Range! I know you're in there."

"That's Logan."

I start to move from the room and Ranger grabs my hand. "Clothes first," he growls before muttering something under his breath about not letting anyone see me naked.

I can't help grinning at the possessive note in his voice as I slip into one of his t-shirts and my rumpled skirt.

"What the fuck? This is the first time I've taken a day off in twelve years." Ranger says as he yanks open the front door to glare at his brother.

But one look at Logan and it's obvious something is wrong. His face is pale, and his eyes are big. "I know, I know. But there was an accident."

Ranger swears under his breath. "Was anyone hurt?"

"Two of our ranch hands. Ethan is with them at the hospital. I figured you'd want to ride down there."

Ranger turns to me. "I could be gone for a few hours."

I nod. "I'll be fine here."

He looks like he doesn't want to leave, but he presses a kiss to my lips and tells me he'll call me when he can.

When he's gone, I walk around the house. It feels emptier without him here, so I decide to go into the office. Even though I don't know how to do a lot, I have a feel for a few of his daily tasks. I can get those accomplished.

The hours until I hear from Ranger pass slowly. When I do, his call is short and garbled. I can't make out much of what he says other than the fact that he's on his way home. I tell him that I'll be waiting for him and shut down.

At the house, I try to read. But my shiny new collection isn't enough to distract me from anticipating Ranger's return. So I decide to make a batch of my favorite fudge brownies while I wait for him.

There's a noise on the porch as I'm mixing the batter and I call out that it's open. I turn at the sound of footsteps, expecting to see my hunky husband and his brothers. But the man standing in the doorway of the kitchen is the one I only ever see in my nightmares now. My father.

My knees turn to jelly and my tongue clings to the roof of my mouth.

He swaggers in like he owns this place, like he owns me. "Took me a while to find you, *Tia*."

I should act. I should scream or call Ranger or do *something*. But I can't. Just like when I was a little kid, I freeze in the monster's presence.

"This is a good little gig you got going here. Convinced some backwoods cowboy to marry you. But you're just as dumb as you ever were." He laughs. "Your stupid hick husband hasn't realized you aren't really his."

He's lying to me. He has to be. Then clarity hits. Of course, he's right. I didn't sign my legal name to the document. I signed a fake name which means Ranger and I aren't married. The man I spent this morning making love to isn't my husband. *He's not mine.* The realization is enough to make my world stop spinning.

My father steps forward, reaching for me.. "It's time for you to come home, Rebecca."

I step away from him before he can connect, bumping my hip on the kitchen counter I've never talked back to my father but today, I shake my head. "I don't want to."

I love this life I'm building here with Ranger. I love his ranch and his home and his body. I love the way he looks at me like I'm the center of the universe and the way he tips his head when he's listening to me. I love the way he makes me feel like everything is going to be OK just by wrapping his strong arms around me.

His smug grin doesn't fade. "Prophet is waiting for you. I talked to him. He's willing to forgive you for this season of folly."

If I know anything about that man, his idea of "forgiveness" will have to be earned after multiple cruel and degrading punishments. An image of my sister's hollow cheeks comes to my mind and strength wells up somewhere from deep inside.

"No." It's the first time I've ever defied my father, but I've spent enough time with him to know what to do next. I duck the coming blow and skirt the counter.

"You'll come with me right now!" He roars.

"I said no!" I shout the words, surprised by how powerful they make me feel.

My father's face contorts with fury and mottles, turning a shade of purple. In this moment I know that he'll have to drag me back. I'm not leaving my Ranger's side, no matter what. "You stupid—"

"She said no," Ranger's voice is filled with a cold rage I've never heard before. It sends a shiver down my back. I didn't even hear him come in the kitchen but now he's sitting there with Logan and Ethan behind him. They look just as furious.

Ranger flicks his attention to me. He scans me, looking for signs that I've been hurt. The expression of concern has me wanting to fling myself into his arms. Instead, I stay where I am. I know better than to give up ground in front of this monster.

My father gives Ranger a smile that doesn't reach his eyes. He might not like my husband, but he's another man. That means he's at least worthy of some respect and a civil conversation. "She's mine. You can't blame a man for wanting his daughter back."

"I can blame you for raising her in a fuckin' cult that taught her she wasn't worthy of kindness and love," Ranger spits out. This is a different side to my man. If I thought he was angry with Declan, it's nothing compared to the fury that surrounds him now.

"She's my property. I'll do as I want."

My heart breaks at his words. That's the way he's

treated me and my sisters our whole lives. We were never humans to him. Just objects that he owned and could trade to better his standing within the community.

"She's not your property, you bastard. She's a grown woman and if she wants to stay or go, that's her decision."

He looks to me then, clearly waiting for me to decide what happens next. It's what sets him apart from my father and all the men I grew up around. Ranger is giving me a choice, a rare and precious gift I've never been granted. This time, I do cross the room. I stand beside him. My voice doesn't shake when I say, "I don't want to go with him."

His gaze flicks back to my father. "Then it's time for you to leave. Escort him out."

Ethan and Logan advance but my father holds up his hands. "There are things you don't know. She's not your legal wife and she signed that marriage contract when she was just seventeen. It's null and void."

The men freeze and wait for Ranger. That's when I realize my mistakes too late. There's nothing legally to hold me here. Ranger could send me away right now. He might decide he doesn't want me after all.

He glances at me, a note of urgency in his voice. "Are you eighteen now?"

I nod, my heart pounding.

"Were you when you signed the marriage certificate using the fake name?"

Another nod. There's a lump in my throat and I have to will myself to swallow it. Whatever happens, I won't cry. I won't give my father the satisfaction of seeing how miserable he's made me.

Ranger turns his attention to my father. "She's an adult. You can't remove her from this place against her will."

"I'll pay you," my father insists. "She's still worth a lot to Prophet. He wants the complete collection."

"Get him out of my sight!" Ranger roars the words to his brothers. They waste no time dragging my father from the house and into the cold January snow.

I listen to my father shouting as they pull him away. He's spouting something about God avenging him for this wrong done.

With him gone, all of my strength and bravado leaves. My legs turn to liquid, but Ranger catches me, pulling me into his lap. "I'm here. You did good. You stood up for yourself."

I search his gaze but find only concern in it. "Are

you angry with me? For the marriage thing? I swear, I didn't think about the fact that it wouldn't be legal just because I signed a different name."

He cups my face. "In my eyes, you're my wife, Tia. I love you."

Tears slip down my cheeks. "I can stay here?"

"Your place will always be right next to me, butterfly," he whispers as he wipes away my tears with his thumb. "Now, let's get this thing done right."

Despite the fact that the courthouse is closed, Ranger makes a few calls and suddenly Judge Helen is there. He explains what happened briefly and she seems happy to help make our marriage legal.

Afterwards, we go home together and spend the rest of the night making love. We pause only to nap for a few minutes at a time before we're reaching for each other again. This man means the world to me, and knowing that he loves me is all I need.

11
TIA

"Were your ranch hands OK?" I ask Ranger after breakfast the next morning. In all of the chaos of what happened with my father last night, I forgot about the fact that he went to the hospital to be with his men.

"They'll be fine. Minor injuries from ignoring safety protocols we have in place. Could have been a lot worse," he tells me as he dries the plates. I love being here with him and washing the dishes together.

He never acts like any of the chores are mine simply because I'm his wife. Instead, he views us as teammates. I've learned that he doesn't mind folding laundry but for some reason, he hates putting it in.

So I load the washer and dry the clothes while he folds them.

"I heard you tell your brothers you were taking today off," I say as I pass him the final dish to dry.

Mischief sparks in his gaze. "I told them not to bother us for a couple of days. Figured we could spend the time getting to know each other better."

I can't help glancing at his full lips. He's so sexy and he's looking at me like getting to know each other better will definitely involve fewer clothes. Not that I care to complain. Ranger is incredibly giving, always making sure he takes care of me before he comes.

There's a knock on the door and he groans before wheeling over to it. He grumps to Logan as soon as he sees him, "Do you not understand the concept of vacation time?"

I don't understand why Logan is here. He was supposed to be picking up his mail-order bride today. If the rumors in town are true about Logan's tendency to sleep around, I would have guessed that he'd be spending the day in bed with his new wife.

Logan scowls at him. "You're the one who put the family things in storage. Where is the key?"

"I have it around here somewhere." Ranger

gestures for his brother to follow him into the house. He tells him to wait in the living room while he goes to find the key, leaving me alone with the normally jovial cowboy.

"How did the wedding go, Logan?" I do my best to give him a smile. I still feel awkward around Ranger's brothers because I don't know them that well. But Logan was one of the men who dragged my father out of the office.

Ranger said that Logan drove my dad to the state border to make sure he wouldn't come back again. He also made it clear to the ranch hands at the gate that anyone matching my father's description must have pre-approval to be let on the grounds.

"Went great," Logan mutters, seemingly distracted.

Ranger returns with the key, passing it to him. "What do you need from storage so urgently?"

"A crib."

He stops his chair. "Things don't happen that fast."

"I need a crib. Figure the one that's been passed down will do just fine. My woman showed up with a baby on her hip," Logan explains, placing his Stetson back on his head as he stands.

"And you married her anyway?" I ask. This doesn't sound like the man that half the town describes. I can't help but wonder if the gossip mill has him all wrong.

Logan doesn't bother glancing my way. He focuses all of his attention on his brother. "You should have seen them, Range. Two sets of scared little eyes."

"I hope you know what you're getting yourself into."

I glare at Ranger. I know he's worried for his brother. But this was us just three days ago, complete strangers who found our way to each other. Maybe it'll be the same for Logan and his new wife. "We'll be here if you need anything."

For the first time since he arrived, Logan smiles. It's a warm one that reaches his eyes. "Thanks for that. Might take you up on it."

When he's gone, Ranger squeezes my hand. "There's something I want to show you on your bookshelf."

"Is this about the books you added to the collection?" I didn't even take time to thumb through them. I just added them to the shelves by the author's name. As it is, I imagine I have more books now than I'll be able to read in my lifetime. But I'll definitely give it my best try.

"You'll have to follow me to find out," he teases. He's already promised to take me to the bookstore any time I want to go. Oh, and the truck. He's going to teach me to drive the truck.

Once we're in my bedroom that I've decided to convert to a library, he scans the bookcases before finding one of the books. It has a giant flower on it, and he passes it to me. "I picked this one because it has pictures."

I don't know anything about gardening but if Ranger is interested in it, I'm more than willing to learn.

I flip open the book to a random spot but what I'm greeted with is most certainly not a flower. It's a man and a woman in the middle of a sex act. "This has nothing to do with botany."

He shrugs. "It's about positions and tips. Figured we could explore some of the stuff in there together. Might be a fun way to kill our time off."

I page through the book, my cheeks warm. I stop on an image that captures me. This one is beautiful and sensual. "What about this one?" I show him the book.

He makes a low growl that has my stomach flipping in a delicious way. Something tells me we're going to have a lot of fun today.

"Let's give it a try," he says right as he scoops me into his arms and wheels me back to our bedroom. This cowboy may not have been what I expected but he's exactly what I needed and he's all mine.

EPILOGUE

TIA

"Alright, what are we voting for?" I step away from the wall and inspect the two colors. We have the choice between snuggly duckling yellow or gentle forest green.

It's been six months since I married Ranger and we're expecting our first child together in four months. I rub my hand across my belly that's getting a little rounder each day. Even though I don't like the weight gain, Ranger certainly doesn't mind. He talks to my stomach every morning, always telling his daughter how much he loves her.

Lydia, my second sister, looks between the two paint samples that I added to the wall. "I'm partial to forest green."

"It is soothing," Naomi, my oldest sister, agrees.

They found me a few weeks after I married Ranger for the second time. It turns out that Lydia left not long after I did. She managed to find Naomi in Asheville but neither of them could locate me until my marriage certificate had my true name on it.

The two of them share an apartment together with Naomi's little girls. All those years I thought she went missing when in reality, she'd taken her kids and disappeared. She'd been careful to make it look like an accident near the river and even after all this time, Prophet has never questioned it.

Naomi seems to have adjusted well. I don't know if it's because she has kids that she has to be strong for or simply because she's been out of the community longer.

I study the green color. I can't describe how happy I am that my sisters are here to do ordinary things with me, like paint the nursery. The only thing that would make me happier is if Sarah were here to help us. But she's eight months pregnant and wasn't up for traveling. Instead, I'll video call her later and show her what we've done to the room. "We'll go with that one then."

"Let's do it," Lydia agrees. Her breath doesn't smell of alcohol today the way it normally does.

She's had a hard time coming to the outside. Not only did Lydia believe in a lot of what she was taught but she's also infertile. She hasn't said much about it, but I'm certain that Prophet made her pay for that.

She takes the paint chip from me and the keys to the car while Naomi and I add painter's tape to the nursery.

"She seems better today," I say when Naomi and I have worked in silence for a few minutes. I know that Naomi wouldn't let her drive if she thought she had been drinking. We might be grown but Naomi still squawks over us like we're little baby birds.

"The outpatient treatment program is really helping her," my older sister explains as she pauses to smooth tape around the edges of the window. It's hard to believe that this used to be my room when I first came here. Now we're going to make it into a nursery.

"I remember she applied. I didn't know she'd gotten approved," I answer. Normally, they tell me about things like this.

"I thought you knew." She nods when she's happy with her taping job. "Ranger is paying for it. There's no way either of us could afford it."

Somehow, I'm not surprised that my sweet husband is doing that. When my sisters first reached out to me, it was obvious they were struggling financially. They didn't ask for a cent even though they were facing eviction from the tiny apartment where they were living.

Without telling me, Ranger made plans to move them into a bigger apartment and paid for the first two years of rent. Even my sisters wouldn't have known who the anonymous benefactor was if the landlord hadn't slipped up and told them.

He also helped Naomi find a good-paying job as a receptionist at a car dealership. She's saving to go to night school though she's sworn me to secrecy. We both know that if Ranger finds out, he'll make that happen too. The way he takes care of my sisters as if they were his own family is just one more reason I love that man.

When Lydia returns with the paint, we get to work on the nursery. While we work, we chat and laugh. For a few hours, it feels like we're normal, like our lives weren't stolen from us by a cult leader.

I've just finished the last swipe of paint when I hear the familiar whirl of Ranger's chair. Like some people recognize their loved one's footsteps, I recognize the sound of his various chairs.

"Dammit, Tia, I told you to be careful." His hands

are around my hips as he tugs me off the step stool and into his lap.

He's always protective over me but with the pregnancy, he's gone into overdrive. He insisted on driving me into town yesterday when I needed a new set of maternity bras. The man would wrap me and our unborn child in bubble wrap if I let him.

I press a kiss to his lips, not caring that my sisters are still in the room. They know I love my husband. While Lydia has said she never wants to get married again, I see the way that Naomi looks when I'm with Ranger. She wants a good husband. I keep telling her to move to the ranch with me. Rough and rugged cowboys who love their women fiercely abound in Courage County.

Since we're finished with the painting, Naomi says, "We need to go. I still have to pick up the munchkins for dinner."

"I can do that, and all of you can crash here tonight," Ranger offers. He's made it clear to them over the past few months that our home is their home. Sometimes, they do take him up on the offer and spend the night. But he never complains when they're around. He's welcomed my sisters with open arms since day one.

She waves her hand. "Another night. They have summer camp to get to in the morning."

I walk them to the door and the three of us exchange a flurry of hugs before they're gone, and I'm left alone with my handsome husband.

"How are we going to fill this long, lonely night?" I ask, sexy ideas filling my mind. Since we've been married, I've discovered a new side to myself. A flirty side that Ranger seems to appreciate just as much as I do. Every time we're together, it feels magical and special. He says that's because we're in love. I say it's because he's so selfless and gentle.

Disappointment flickers across Ranger's face. "Logan and Audrey are coming for dinner."

I'd forgotten about that. We normally eat dinner with Logan and his wife at least once a week. They have a great marriage and the cutest little daughter, Paisley. I love cuddling with the one-year-old. It reminds me that soon I'm going to get to meet my own daughter.

I shower while Ranger throws together a quick meal that we eat on the patio while watching the July sun slowly sink lower.

Dinner is a simple affair. Logan and Ranger talk about the ranch while Audrey and I discuss motherhood. She's been an invaluable source of information since I found out I was pregnant. She's the first person outside of Ranger that I told.

When dinner is done and our family has finally left, my husband pulls me into our bedroom for some alone time.

"I have a surprise for you," I tell him, the lacy material that's been caressing me all night is definitely damp at this point. Every time it brushed against me during the meal, I could only think about how much fun he and I would be having soon.

"I have one for you," he says, a twinkle in his eye. Ranger enjoys finding things to do for me. Whether it's adding a new book to my collection or giving me a foot rub, he's always expressing his love for me in different ways.

"You go first," I tell him. The moment he sees what I have on underneath my sundress that we're both going to forget everything else.

"It's in my dresser drawer," he says.

I retrieve a white box with a ribbon tied around it. I rattle it and listen for the sound because I've learned that he hates it when I try to guess the gift. There's no sound with this one.

He smirks at me. "Finally found one that you couldn't guess."

"Are you going to tell me what it is?" I ask as I

sink onto the edge of our bed. My pregnancy has been great. I've had a very easy one compared to some women and I'm so thankful for that.

"Open it and see," he prompts before joining me on the bed.

I wait for him to get settled then open the box. What greets me is a paper print-out. It's reservations for that bed and breakfast in South Carolina I mentioned to him a few weeks ago. "Aww, you remembered."

"Course I did." He presses a kiss to the crown of my head. "I think we should go now. You know, the honeymoon we never took."

I can't help smiling. He is determined to give me everything I ever wanted. I could tell him I want the moon, and he'd start making plans to get it for me. This man is endlessly thoughtful. Now it's time to show him that I'm thoughtful too.

"Are you ready for your surprise?" I ask as I shimmy off the bed. One of the things that I've loved about the pregnancy is that it makes me horny all the time. Not that Ranger ever complains. He's more than happy to love on my body. Just like he promised, he worships me every day and we're still discovering new things together.

He nods and I step back further so he can appreciate the surprise. Then I reach for the tie on my wraparound sundress and undo it.

To tease him, I slowly peel the dress apart and let it drop from my shoulders onto the floor. Now, I'm standing before him in only my hot pink lacy undergarments.

Lust fills Ranger's expression and his eyes turn to liquid fire. "I like your surprise better than mine."

I can't help but laugh as I strut toward the bed, putting an extra sway in my hips. "I thought you might."

An hour later when I'm exhausted and sweaty, I snuggle into Ranger's embrace. He rubs my arm and grins. "You're going to be a great mom, butterfly."

The words warm me as I place a hand over my belly. "I can't wait to meet her."

"We will soon," he reassures me.

I can't help smiling at his promise. I had no idea the day I applied to become a mail-order bride that my life would change forever. That day, I didn't just find a groom. I found the man that's meant to be mine.

READ NEXT: THE COWBOY'S SOULMATE

Can a jaded playboy find forever with his curvy mail order bride and her baby? Or will her past ruin their future?

Logan

The town calls me Love 'Em and Leave 'Em Logan.

Growing up as a foster kid, I figured out quick that if I'm the first to say goodbye then it doesn't hurt. After all, nothing lasts forever. That's why I'm not looking forward to my upcoming wedding.

In order to secure my place as a Scott heir and finally be a member of a real family, I have to get married and quick. My late grandfather already put everything in motion by finding me a mail order bride.

But when I show up to claim my woman, she's carrying the mother of all surprises: a little baby girl. One look at two sets of scared eyes and I know that I'll do whatever it takes to protect my girls and make this marriage last.

Audrey

I didn't feel great about lying.

I'm a mail order bride with a baby on my hip. I didn't mention it in the profile because I couldn't risk getting turned away. If what Logan's profile said is true, he's just as desperate to make this marriage work as I am.

But no matter how kind Logan is or how good he is to my daughter, I can't forget that I have a past. A past that could show up at any moment and destroy the little family I'm building with my cowboy husband.

If you're looking for a mail order bride romance with a protective cowboy who fiercely loves a single mom with a baby, then it's time to meet Logan in The Cowboy's Soulmate.

Read Logan and Audrey's Story

COURAGE COUNTY SERIES

Welcome to Courage County where protective alpha heroes fall for strong curvy women they love and defend. There's NO cheating and NO cliffhangers. Just a sweet, sexy HEA in each book.

Love on the Ranch

Her Alpha Cowboy

Pregnant and alone, Riley has nowhere to go until the alpha cowboy finds her. Will she fall in love with her rescuer?

Her Older Cowboy

Summer is making a baby with her brother's best friend. But he insists on making it the old-fashioned way.

Her Protector Cowboy

Jack will do whatever it takes to protect his curvy woman after their hot one-night stand…then he plans to claim her!

Her Forever Cowboy

Dean is in love with his best friend's widow. When they're stranded together for the night, will he finally tell her how he feels?

Her Dirty Cowboy

The ranch's newest hire also happens to be the woman Adam had a one-night stand with…and she's carrying his baby!

Her Sexy Cowboy

She's a scared runaway with a baby. He's determined to protect them both. But neither of them expected to fall in love.

Her Wild Cowboy

He'll keep his curvy woman safe, even if it means a marriage in name only. But what happens when he wants to make it a real marriage?

Her Wicked Cowboy

One hot night with Jake gave me the best gift of my life: a beautiful baby girl. Will he want us to be a family when I show up on his doorstep a year later?

Courage County Brides

The Cowboy's Bride

The only way out of my horrible life is to become a mail order bride. But will my new cowboy husband be willing to take a chance on love?

The Cowboy's Soulmate

Can a jaded playboy find forever with his curvy mail order bride and her baby? Or will her secret ruin their future?

The Cowboy's Valentine

I'm a grumpy loner cowboy and I like it that way. Until my beautiful mail order bride arrives and suddenly, I want more than a marriage in name only.

The Cowboy's Match

Will this mail order bride matchmaker take a chance on love when she falls for the bearded cowboy who happens to be her VIP client?

The Cowboy's Obsession

Can this stalker cowboy show the curvy schoolteacher that he's the one for her?

The Cowboy's Sweetheart

Rule #1 of becoming a mail order bride: never fall in love with your cowboy groom.

The Cowboy's Angel

Can this cowboy single dad with a baby find love with his new mail order bride?

The Cowboy's Heiress

This innocent heiress is posing as a mail order bride. But what happens when her grumpy cowboy husband discovers who she really is?

Courage County Warriors

Rescue Me

Getting out was hard. Knowing who to trust was easy: my dad's best friend. He's the only man I can count on, but will we be able to keep our hands off each other?

Protect Me

When I need a warrior to protect me, I know just who to turn to: my brother's best friend. But will this grumpy cowboy who's guarding my body break my heart?

Shield Me

When trouble comes for me, I know who to call—my ex-boyfriend's dad. He's the only one who can help. But can I convince this grumpy cowboy to finally claim me?

Courage County Fire & Rescue

The Firefighter's Curvy Nanny

As a single dad firefighter, I was only looking for a quick fling. Then the curvy woman from last night shows up. Turns out, she's my new nanny.

The Firefighter's Secret Baby

After a scorching one-night stand with a sexy firefighter, I realize I'm pregnant…with my brother's best friend's baby.

The Firefighter's Forbidden Fling

I knew a one night stand with my grumpy boss wasn't the best idea…but I didn't think it would lead to anything serious. I definitely didn't think it would lead to a surprise pregnancy with this sexy firefighter.

GET A FREE COWBOY ROMANCE

Get Her Grumpy Cowboy for FREE:
https://www.MiaBrody.com/free-cowboy/

LIKE THIS STORY?

If you enjoyed this story, please post a review about it. Share what you liked or didn't like. It may not seem like much, but reviews are so important for indie authors like me who don't have the backing of a big publishing house.

Of course, you can also share your thoughts with me via email if you'd prefer to reach out that way. My email address is mia @ miabrody.com (remove the spaces). I love hearing from my readers!

ABOUT THE AUTHOR

Mia Brody writes steamy stories about alpha men who fall in love with big, beautiful women. She loves happy endings and every couple she writes will get one!

When she's not writing, Mia is searching for the perfect slice of cheesecake and reading books by her favorite instalove authors.

Keep in touch when you sign up for her newsletter: https://www.MiaBrody.com/news. It's the fastest way to hear about her new releases so you never miss one!

Printed in Great Britain
by Amazon